To Jonathan!

Baghead

For Lynn and Holly

All rights reserved. Published in the United States by Dragonfly Books, an imprint of Random House Children's Books, a division of Random House, Inc., New York. Originally published in hardcover in the United States by Alfred A. Knopf, an imprint of Random House Children's Books, a division of Random House, Inc., New York, in 2002.

Dragonfly Books with the colophon is a registered trademark of Random House, Inc.

Visit us on the Web! www.randomhouse.com/kids

Educators and librarians, for a variety of teaching tools, visit us at www.randomhouse.com/teachers

Library of Congress Cataloging-in-Publication Data
Krosoczka, Jarrett.
Baghead / by Jarrett J. Krosoczka.
p.   cm.
Summary: Josh hides under a bag on his head, until his sister has a better idea.
ISBN 978-0-375-81566-9 (trade) — ISBN 978-0-375-91566-6 (lib. bdg.)
ISBN 978-0-553-11172-9 (pbk.)
[1. Hair—Fiction. 2. Haircutting—Fiction. 3. Humorous stories.] I. Title.
PZ7.K935 Bag 2002
[E]—dc21   2001038138

MANUFACTURED IN CHINA

16 15 14 13 12 11 10

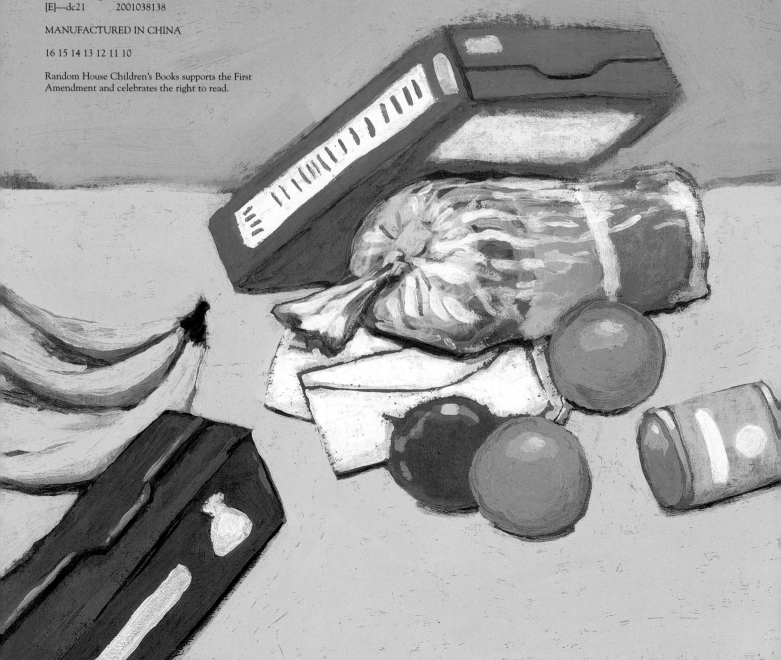

Baghead

Jarrett J. Krosoczka

Dragonfly Books —— New York

On
wednesday
morning,
Josh had
an **idea**.

A very **BIG** idea.

A very **BROWN** idea.

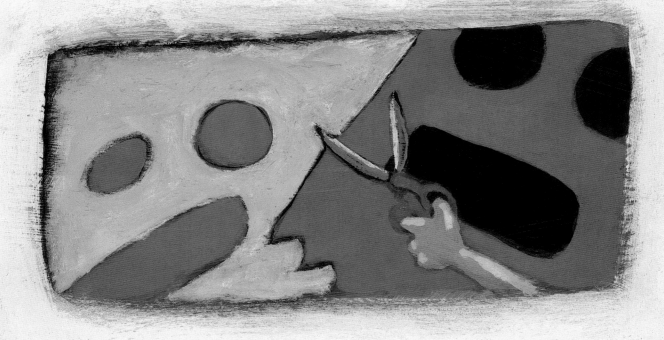

A very **BIG,**
BROWN,
BAG idea.

Josh thought it was a good idea.

His mother did not.

"You can't eat breakfast with a paper **bag** on your head!"

she said.

But JOSH did.

He piled a forkful of scrambled eggs into his mouth and didn't leave a crumb on his plate.

His bus driver, Mrs. Boyle,
opened the door
and stared at him.

"You crazy kid!
You can't go to
school like
that!"

she exclaimed.

But Josh climbed on the bus
and rode to school.

His teacher, Mr. Tucker,
wasn't amused.

"Don't tell me
you **forgot**
your
book report,"

he said.

JOSH didn't. He stood in front of the class and told them about a boy who met a giant slug.

His soccer coach, MS. O'Neil, frowned.

"How do you plan to play like **that?**"

she demanded.

"with my feet," JOSH said,
and scored three goals.

His dad picked him up
after the game.

"was it
crazy-hat
day
at school?"

he asked.

"Nope," said Josh.

At dinner, his mother didn't say anything. Neither did his brother or his dad.

"Why are you wearing a bag, Josh?" his little sister asked.

"Because I tried to cut my own hair," said Josh.

On Thursday morning, Josh's sister had an **idea.**

A very **COOL** idea.

A very SPIKY idea.

A very **COOL,**
SPIKY,
MEGA-HOLD GEL
idea.